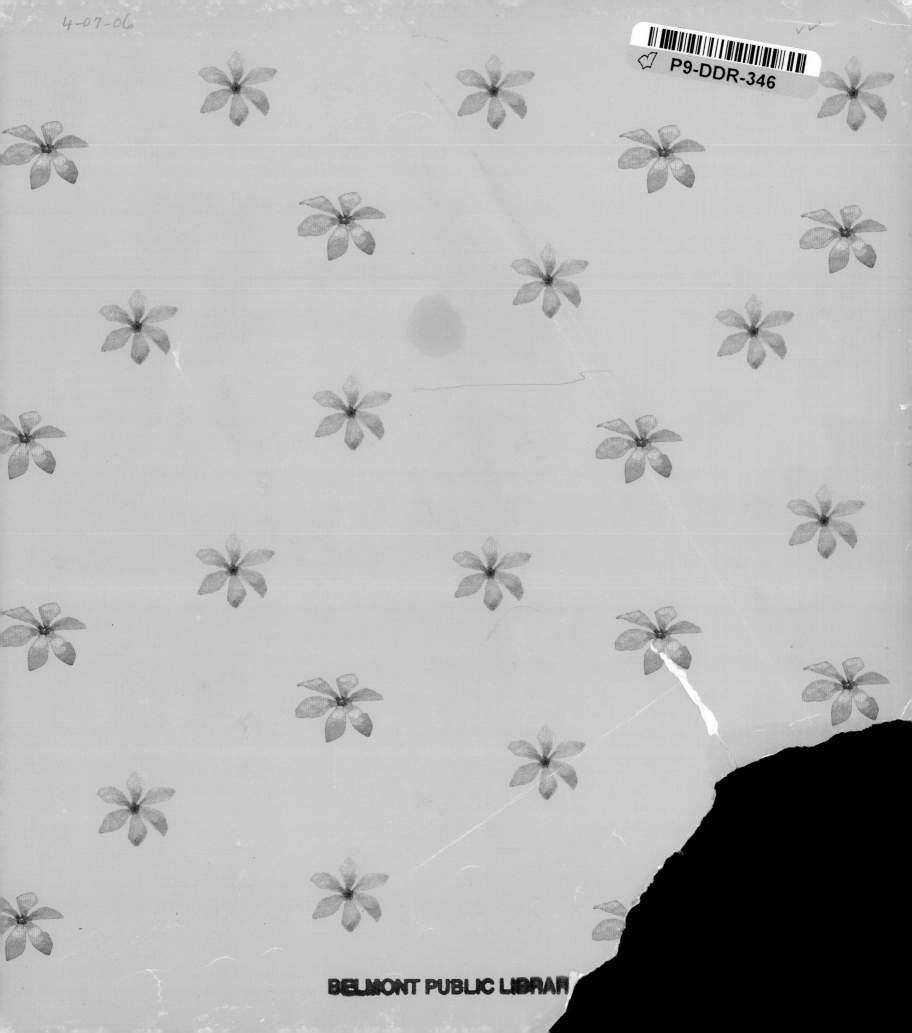

I Love It When You Smile

Text copyright © 2005 by Sam McBratney

Illustrations copyright © 2005 by Charles Fuge

Manufactured in China.

Library of Congress Cataloging-in-Publication Data

McBratney, Sam.

[It's lovely when you smile]

I love it when you smile / Sam McBratney ; [illustrated by] Charles Fuge.— 1st U.S. ed.

p. cm.

Originally published in Great Britain in 2005 under title: It's lovely when you smile.

Summary: A grumpy little kangaroo is having a bad day until his mother finds a way to make him smile.

ISBN-10: 0-06-084245-8

ISBN-13: 978-0-06-084245-1

[1. Smile—Fiction. 2. Kangaroos—Fiction.] I. Fuge, Charles, ill. II. Title.

PZ7.M47826Its 2006    2005005730    [E]—dc22    CIP    AC

1 2 3 4 5 6 7 8 9 10

Originally published in Great Britain as *It's Lovely When You Smile* by Puffin Books

First U.S. Edition, HarperCollins Publishers, 2006

# I Love It When You Smile

Sam McBratney
Charles Fuge

HarperCollins*Publishers*

It was a lovely summer morning,
but Roo was feeling grumpy
and he didn't know why.

He was feeling so grumpy that
he didn't even want to play.

"What's wrong with you this morning?" asked his mother.

"Nothing," said Roo.

"You should smile," his mother said. "Everybody feels better when they smile."

But Little Roo wasn't in a smiling mood today,
not even when his mother tickled him gently.
"Did I see a tiny smile?" she asked.
"Just one?"

"No!" said Roo.
"You didn't."

It was the kind of game that little kangaroos love to play!

His mom reached out and flipped him up head over heels.

But would it work this grumpy morning?

No. Little Roo did **not** smile.

Not even a teeny-weeny bit.

His mother **skipped** into a hollow

tree where they liked to **play**.

She popped her head through

a hole in the trunk.

"**Smile!**"

"I still don't want to," said Little Roo.

"Oh dear," said his mom.
So she gathered up
some dry leaves,
tossed them
into the air,
and all the leaves
came down on
Little Roo.

He looked **so** funny!
"I think I can see a **smile** this time,"
his mom said, and **laughed**.
"Just a little
one . . .?"

"You don't," said Roo. "I'm NOT smiling."
"Oh well," his mother said with a sigh.

It was time for breakfast.
Little Roo's mom lifted him up. "Let's go down
the hill together and find something to eat."
"I'm not hungry," said Roo grumpily.
"But I'm hungry," said his mom.
"Come on."

"Hold on tight!"

And off they went.

Halfway down the hill there was a hole.

It wasn't a deep hole, but it was a wide hole,

and a **muddy-at-the-bottom** hole.

"Look out!" cried Roo.

But his mom was doing silly hops

from side to side instead

of looking

where

she

was

going

AND . . .

...slippity

...slippity

...slide

and...

What a mess.
WHAT A
MESS!

Roo himself was muddy all over.
Then he looked at his mother, who was soaking wet and
slimy from the tops of her ears to the tips of her toes.

And Little Roo couldn't do anything else.

He just
had
to . . .

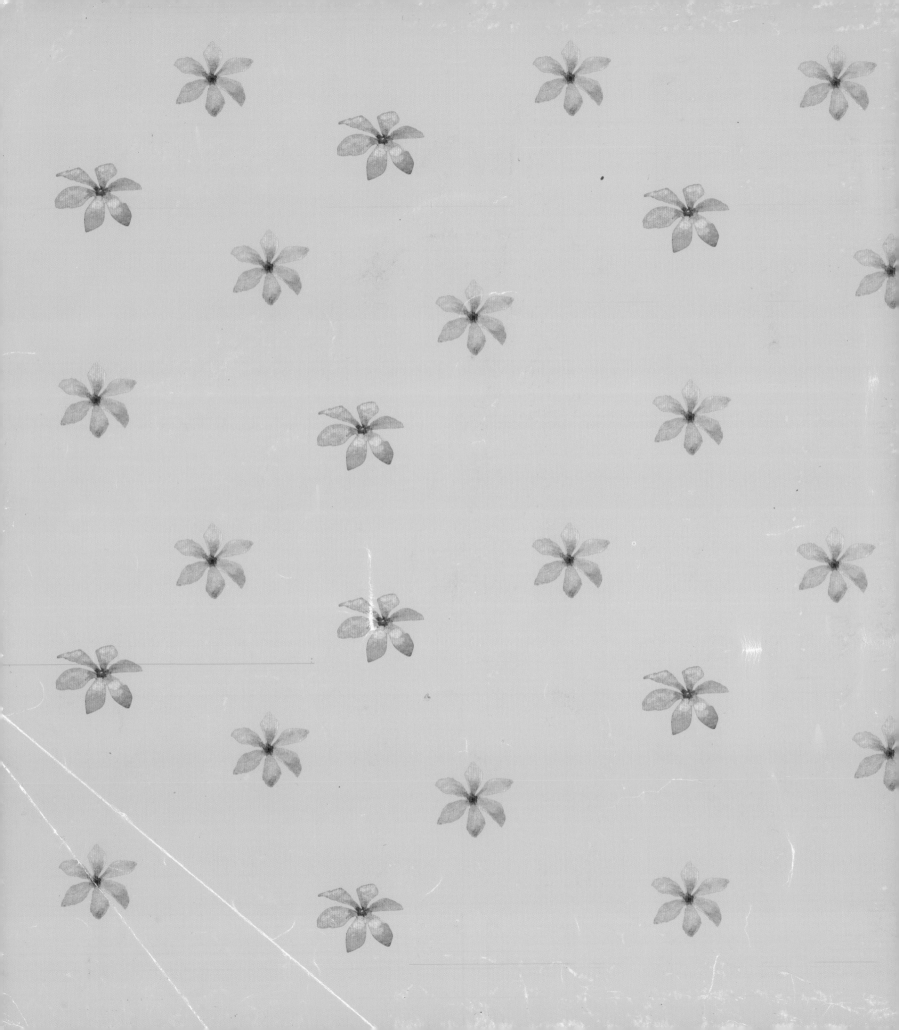